This dinosaur belongs to:

. . . .

Titanosaurs are the largest known animals ever to have walked the earth. This story is inspired by the discovery of the biggest type of titanosaur ever discovered. The giant bones were found in Argentina in 2014.

The biggest known titanosaur was longer than four London buses.

It would have weighed more than ten African elephants!

Gabby Dawnay

Alex Barrow

if I had a dinosaur

I do like

I've got a

A is far too wet.

Because you see, I really want a different sort of pet.

I thought about a

 I thought about a

But I want a pet much bigger,
more the size of, well,

A HOUSE!

I really want a giant pet, enormous, big and strong, with a body broad and solid, and a tail that's super long.

Oh if I had a **DINOSAUR**

I'd teach him lots of tricks,
like how to roll and how to sit
and fetch and carry sticks!

If I had a dinosaur, I'd walk him in the park.

I wonder if my dinosaur would roar?

Or would he bark?

If I had a dinosaur, he'd carry me to school
and all my friends would shout, "Oh wow!

Your dinosaur is cool!"

My dinosaur would learn to count and say the alphabet ...

... and all the teachers would declare,

"Why,
what a clever pet!"

Dinosaurs need water
(I think they like to swim)

I'd have to dig a massive pond
and fill it to the brim.

If I had a dinosaur,
I'd feed him lots of greens,
like cabbages and broccoli
to keep him full of beans!

Dinosaurs make smashing pets,
as dinosaurs can do
much better stuff than dogs or cats.

Just watch out for the ...

If I had a dinosaur,
I'd get a "dino-flap,"

so he could come inside my house
and take a little nap.

Our sofa is enormous,
it's big enough for four.
Just perfect for a sleepy sort
of friendly dinosaur.

I wish I had a dinosaur,
to cuddle up at night,
to read a bedtime story with
and give my dad a fright!

Yes, dinosaurs make awesome pets,
I'm sure you will agree
that of all the pets they are the best —
just get one and you'll see!

For Mimi, Olla, Kip and Frank - G. D.

For my son Kasper - A. B.

With thanks to Sir David Attenborough, whose
BBC documentary *Attenborough and the Giant
Dinosaur* brought this enormous discovery to life.

First published in the United States of America in 2017 by
Thames & Hudson Inc., 500 Fifth Avenue, New York, New York 10110

Reprinted 2021

Library of Congress Control Number 2016941849

ISBN 978–0–500–65099–8

Printed and bound in China by Everbest Printing Co. Ltd

Be the first to know about our new releases,
exclusive content and author events by visiting
thamesandhudson.com
thamesandhudsonusa.com
thamesandhudson.com.au